Belle's Love Story

adapted by **Kristine Lombardi**
illustrated by the **Disney Storybook Artists**

Reader's
Digest
Children's Books®

New York, New York • Montréal, Québec • Bath, United Kingdom

When Belle first agreed to stay at the castle with the Beast so her father could go free, she didn't know if she had made the right decision.

All of the enchanted objects in the castle tried to make her feel at home, but Belle had given up all her dreams of adventure. The castle was her home now.

Belle is sad the first night in the castle. Look in your mirror and make a sad face.

And Belle didn't think she'd ever get along with the Beast. She thought he was mean. Plus, he was always angry!

The Beast has a short temper! Look in your mirror and make your best angry face!

But eventually, she got to know the real Beast. They spent a lot of time together, and she saw a different side of him. He was actually very sweet and kind.

And then, one day, the Beast asked Belle to join him for a special dinner. Belle realized that the Beast was trying to do something nice for her.

She wanted to look perfect. Wardrobe and Mrs. Potts helped her choose a beautiful gown to wear.

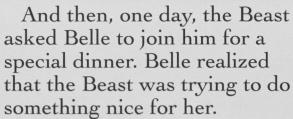

Put on your prettiest dress then look in the mirror.

Babette, the feather duster, helped her decide on the perfect hairstyle.

Belle knew it was going to be a very special night.

Brush your hair into a fancy style to go with a fancy gown!

While she was getting ready, the Beast was, too! Lumiere and Cogsworth helped him choose the perfect outfit, and they came up with a new hairstyle for him.

How would the Beast do his hair?

Belle came down the stairs and the Beast was waiting for her at the bottom. He told her that she looked beautiful—and she felt beautiful! It was going to be a wonderful evening.

Look in the mirror and smile like Belle when she sees the Beast in the ballroom.

The new friends had a delicious dinner and danced around the ballroom. And after they danced, they went out on to the balcony and breathed in the beautiful scent of roses.

Dance the way Belle does, but use your brush to make sure your hair looks great after all that twirling!

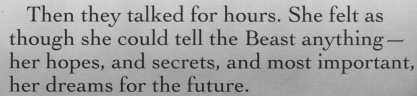

Then they talked for hours. She felt as though she could tell the Beast anything— her hopes, and secrets, and most important, her dreams for the future.

Belle still longed for adventure and excitement. And somehow she knew that her future would include the Beast.